# Tears of the Heart

## Shirleyann Regis

authorHOUSE®

*AuthorHouse*™
*1663 Liberty Drive*
*Bloomington, IN 47403*
*www.authorhouse.com*
*Phone: 1-800-839-8640*

*First published by AuthorHouse     2/18/2010*

*ISBN: 978-1-4389-9376-8 (sc)*

*Printed in the United States of America*
*Bloomington, Indiana*

*This book is printed on acid-free paper.*

A special thanks to my friends and loved ones for believing in me.

*To the Heart*

# THE PROMISE

My sweetheart the lights has gone out on
 this part of our story but I am still lost in
our love. Sweetheart I remember you love
candles, you always said how beautiful you
 felt by candle light, so I will continue
lighting candles to keep you close and keep
the promise we made to each other. "I said I am
yours and you said you are mine." I live to
feel the warm touch of your hands on mine
 again. "My love how I missed the sweet taste
of your lips On mine." I can feel you around
me, I am so much in love with you my
 darling. I know I should let you go but I am
lost without you. My love you are everything
to me, my heart will always be yours. I feel
 your presence with every breath I take, you
are so much a part of me, my wish is to be
with you. "Many say I am a dreamer, and
maybe I am, but I can still hear your sweet
calling. I understand now what everlasting
love truly means. "I love you my darling
 please hold the door open for me, I want to
be lost in your arms again."

# THE RETURN

Return to me! Was his request and I asked
why? He replied saying "You know why."
His voice was so familiar, I remembered feeling
beautiful and cherished from his soft
touched. "Do you remember us?" I replied "Yes
it felt like coming home." "Can you remember
my face my love?" He asked
My response was I can't, I do remember
being loved by you. "Do you believe the
love you felt came from my heart?" he asked
"Yes, I believe I have always known your
love." I replied
I love you, he declared... "Will you return to
me?" I replied... I am on my way.

# FIRST KISS

I am waiting for the sweetest kiss, that
earth shattering kiss when time stands
still. There is no mistaking this kiss
existence, it's a moment that should be
embraced with no questioned. This kiss
confirms the essence of love, young or old
we all crave it. We want to lose ourselves
in the wonders of this amazing moment
it's beyond words and so sensuous, the first
feeling of another's lips against yours is
truly divine.

# CHRISTMAS MORNING

Feeling my love's touch felt like
Christmas morning, the feeling of
Christmas always made my heart
sing. My love placed the softest kisses
on my fingers and continued to my lips
as he pulled me in his arms in the month
of May, I am so in love with him, how I
wish I could have Christmas morning
everyday of the year, for I enjoyed the
warm feeling of our love and his
wonderful touch which reminds me
of a beautiful Christmas morning.

# THE SEARCH

Love should come easy, a look, a kiss
a touch being together should make
passion scream out loud, losing yourselves
in each other should be lovely, looking
into each others eyes should set the soul
on fire, whispering words of longing
should say that this is love. It should
ignite all the senses of passion, sharing
these feelings over and over again
should simply be beautiful. Whispering
the words "I love you" should be
believable, but fulfillment did not
make her presence known in this search so
the search continues.

# BUTTERFLY

He called her his butterfly, and from
a distance she was, he could be one
with her, get lost in the wonders of
her beauty. She was a free spirit, this
he knew to be true. There were moments
when he wished he could hold her and
admire her beautiful colors up close, but
he knew if his longing wish came true
he would lose his love, her beautiful
wings would fold and so would her free
spirit which captured him from the
moment he saw her, knowing this he
made a choice to admire her from a far.

# SURRENDER

I surrender my love... I surrender to
the thought of knowing I am lost
without you... I surrender to the
thought of knowing that you can
say the most simple words and I will
melt. I surrender... For one kiss from
you makes me feel I can fly. I
surrender... For you take my breath
away. I surrender... For I know we
are meant to be together... So my
love accept my vow... I surrender.

# SEE ME

If you say it's possible, I will be
at your side forever, I know your
heart is full of love, it's the
purest one I have ever known, your
ability to love without question
moves me. It amazes me that I still
have a place to call my own. When
I look in your eyes, I know why you
love me, your heart sees me with all
my imperfections, my desires and my
strength, your love makes me want
to love you more, beloved you truly do
see me.

# MY DARLING

I want to taste all of you, take
in the warmth of you, I want to
know what makes you smile.
I am lost in the treasure of you.
When you look in my eyes it's
the most breathtaking moment
I have ever felt. "I love you" I
want so much to love all of you
my sweet darling.

## STILL

Can one fall in and out of love?
My love I heard your voice today
and I was there again, remembering
when we met, and how I enjoyed your
lips on mine knowing you could not
stop kissing me, I remembered when we
came undone in each others arms. The
passion we felt still takes me to our
special place... If only I could make
time stand still, I would! Just to feel
your breath on my face or to fall asleep
in your arms again knowing our lips
were only inches apart. "Tell me it
is possible to fall in love all over again?"

# I AM IN LOVE

He wanted her to be the one, the one
he could reach out to, so he waited
only to feel heart break as the years
went by. The deepest sadness was felt
as she kept her heart distant from
him. She was only willing to give him
friendship. Many questions comes to
mind..."Why can't she see that I love
her? Does she know I miss hearing her
voice? Does she knows I need her love?
But questions always give hidden
answers. "I was the only one in love."
he finally said out loud. He smiled
at the realization, and his heart cried.
"This love was never meant to be." He
whispered to himself.

# DESIRE

I have always wanted to be a part
of you and get lost in you, when we
are together I can truly be myself.
I am craving you even more my love
as you hold me in your arms. I love
hearing your voice whispering sweet
words to me, you always know the
words I want to hear, they take me
places that only you could show me
your hands on my skin sets me on fire.
My greatest desire is to be with you
always, how I love getting lost in you.
"My love you are the one that knows
my heart."

# REPEAT PERFORMANCE

She allowed him in... Knowing she
should not! But her heart opened
the door and the look of longing took
over. Lips and hands did the dance
that only lovers do so well, lips
whispered words of desire, time was
helpless with no warning to give, as
the lovers came undone, arms gave
comfort, lips made a repeat performance
words followed as well and arms
embraced again. Dawn came with
the warmth of a breathtaking sunrise
which should have been welcomed, but
lips, arms, and lovers did a disappearing
acted for the sun light was to bright
to bear.

# PARADISE

I dreamt I could feel paradise, in
my dream voices spoke many
languages of love, feelings and ideas
were finally understood. Thoughts
was shared, and received. Love was
given and returned, tears appear but
they were beautiful and loving tears.
We were all equal, and laughter was
welcomed. Young and old share stories
and we all listened with great respect.
We knew only one race. "The human
race" I pray for this wonderful paradise
we are all so gifted in making this
dream come to life. I would like to believe
that this paradise is truly in our hands.
"Are you willing to play your part?"

# NEVER GIVE UP

The doors were opened with the hope
of something new but nothing came.
The windows were also opened waiting
on hope but nothing came, so a new day
was wished upon. Sleep was called upon
but dreams did not appear in the name
of comfort. Sadness showed her goodness
and presented her close companion pain.
The mind gave reasons to hold on, but the
feeling of lost over shadowed the message
and the mind felt powerless. The heart
painted a picture of hope, and continued
showing its strength over the power of
time, it gave reasons why the doors and
windows should always be opened. The
message given was simply... "Never give
up."

# THE ARTIST

If I was a artist I would paint the
ideal family, this great painting
would be breathtaking and very
appealing to the eye. A family
a true family breathes different
personalities and awaken feelings
of love, dreams and challenges.
Families are not perfect but the
love should always be constant
and unconditional. Every member
should see each other's needs, though
judgments are made, the love given
should be with a open heart. If I was
a gifted artist I would paint a picture
of a family with emotional colors
and remarkable personalities. "So I
call on you to be the artist, how would
you paint your family if you could?"

# NEW DAY

A new day... Do you understand
what this means? It's a gifted day.
This is a day to start everything
new, it's a day to make changes
and see the best of you, it's a fresh
start. "Will you make the best of
this day? I hope you will, it's a
new beginning, it counts more than
you realize. How will you be today?
Please take a moment and know
that this is our day, make it a great
day, this is a wonderful experience to
be shared by all.

# DADDY'S GIRL

This angel was given wisdom to
embrace the world, she walks
 with grace, and possesses strength.
I am amazed by her beautiful
 heart. She may allow her weakness
 to be seen by some, but take heart for
when you see her tears you may
want to protect her, but make no
mistake that when this angel
lets you comfort her, she is not weak
or helpless.  This special one is strong
and wise, her schooling came from
one who knows what it takes to
step into the world of life. He is never
to far away when help is needed, he
knows she will always make him
proud, after all she is daddy's girl.

# COMING UNDONE

Lightning strikes and the soul felt
 frightened, rain came offering comfort
 but fear made she presence known.
Help was called upon, screaming the
 words... Comfort me! I am lost! Please
save me! Fears once thought placed at
 rest are now awakened, and confusion
beckon to be acknowledged. Hopelessness
 takes over playing her role beautifully
 as always, another stroke of lightning
 came, and the world seem to have swallowed
this loving soul, leaving hopelessness to
 finally know she has won the battle over
courage.

# MORNING

I awaken to morning with his
arms still wrapped around me
my love made me feel protected.
I knew the warmth of his love
would always be there and fell
asleep again. He kissed me and
took me in, as he did before.
Morning came again and my
love still held me, the feeling of
his love surround me when he
kissed me again and I welcomed
sleep again.

# LOST MOMENTS

Reflecting on happy moments placed
me in time. I remember being your
everything, you always light up when I
walked into a room, when we talked our
love shine through. My precious one, we
had so many special moments. "How did we
lost our way? How did we lose each other?
My heart cries for you every second of
the day. It has always been you and I.
I find myself making plans for us, but
you are not here, the realization pains
me, my love we are losing moments that
can never be replaced for many are
gaining and we are losing, how I love you
my precious one, you own my heart, I
will love you always.

# THE WALK

In a instant darkness felled upon him
the memories he tried desperately to
avoid came rushing back and brought
him to his knees. Everything came all
at once, he could hear her laughter
take in her scent, feel her touch
remember her walk and her smile.
He was not a weak man but he knew
he was lost without her. She was the
voice that guided him, she was his heart.
His sweetheart knew what he needed
before he did. She was his other half, the
best part of him. The darkness he felt
was accepting that his love was gone.
He knew he would have to walk this life
without her, his other half, his loving wife.

## SIENNA

Heaven called with the sweetest
news ever heard ... Embrace
my rose he command! My sweet
Sienna Rose has arrived, be kind
and love her with a open heart.
My sweet one is gifted and special.
She is my beautiful star, with one
smile she will capture your heart.
She is my gift to you, so take care
of my rose. Show her your heart and
she will share her gifts with you.

# HOPE

Angel you have embraced your will
and it's yours, how wonderful it
feels, it seems like a dream come
true, this is your freedom and you are
happy, comfort is given by everyone.
But this new found freedom is a costly
one my precious, for it was built on lies and
betrayal. I wanted to teach you so many
things and guide you, but it was made
clear that my guidance was not needed.
The world has a hold on you now. I can't
make you whole anymore, how I wish
I could. It's up to you to find your way
now, please know that I will always
love you. My arms will always be open
waiting for your return.

# ENVY

They all watched from a distance
claiming to be loving and supportive
but envy was brewing. She didn't
think she was special for she was told
she wasn't, yet she found her way even
through negativity she bloomed into a
beautiful flower, love came her way
and many gifts was given. Those who
claimed to love wanted to be part of her
world and she welcomed them without
question. She didn't see the envy, the
wanting, the games or the opening she
allowed. "Why would she?" she wanted
to believe, and hoped their love would last
but this was all about envy. Envious
eyes was full of wanting, always looking
for a moment of greatness to claim, always
looking to be better or greater. However
envy itself didn't see who also wanted to
play a role in her game, not one moment was
taken to think of anyone, envy was only
driven by her longing of wanting at any cost.

# POSSESSION

A love once so inviting and loving
has possessed her will, this love
controlled her every want, her every
thought. She wanted this love to
answer the simple questions
but they were never answered, this
love only wanted possession of her.
She couldn't remember when it all
started to change. This love's hold
on her was strong, she feared she would
never be able to escape. She knew this
love would never let her go, she had
become its obsession. She was this love's
only reason for living, so she continued
to find a way to free herself, for this was
not love.

# STOLEN DESTINY

We would all like the pieces of life to
fit, for it makes sense when wisdom is
gained, but does wisdom lose it's meaning
when the pieces are made to fit for ones
gain? Some would say you are playing
God, wanting to be something or someone
else is the saddest choice one can make.
This was not yours to have, no matter how
wonderful it feels, playing with lives or
wanting to be fulfilled is hurtful and
beyond selfish, wanting to feel another's joy
beckons a question... Why! How I wish I
could shed a tear for the players of this sad
game, but I simply can't. I can only wish
for this taker of destiny to live their life
and embraced their own destiny.

# READ ME A STORY

She asked him to read to her, and he did
happily, as he read to her she smiled for
she knew this was a special moment.
Listening to his voice as he read was
intoxicating, her love wanted to please
her and he did, with that thought
in mind her heart melt, she felt lost in
time. It was the most sensual moment
she has ever shared with anyone. How
soft and beautiful it all was. His voice
told her of his love and the surrender of
his heart. He became her love that night.
what a loving man he was. Sadly
their moments together was brief but it
will never be forgotten.

# CONSUMED

I took one taste and knew I was lost.
How sweet it was on my lips, taking
it all in for the first time, I became
love captive, and wanted to be part
of this world tonight. Love felt wonderful
against my lips, this sweet adventure
took me to places I always wanted
to visit, I held on to love as it consumed
me, never have I felt so beautiful and
peaceful. Love shared the promise of
happy endings and the beauty of falling
for the first time, I felt helpless as love
consumed me, and gave in to the taste
over and over again.

# MIRROR

There's comfort to be found in the
little things life offers, but these
little things are simply overlooked
avoided one might say. The many
choices we make can bring out the
worst of us. A life once filled with
promise and love has become a distant
memory, so we avoid taking a closer
look. However life's reflection can be
seen through a powerful glass... It's
called a mirror, so many of us avoid
it, not wanting to see what we have
become. Not accepting how empty our
hearts have become, for we all know
that mirrors never lies. So we tell
ourselves that the mirror has never
been a friend and in return we choose
not to look upon it.

# TEARS OF THE HEART

The promise of everlasting love was
spoken, desires beyond belief was felt.
When they became one for the first
time, it was indeed a sweet moment
of surrender. This should have been
their love story, the happily ever
after they dreamt of, but sadly it
wasn't and the heart cried. They were
so close to paradise, this love was good
and special, but time moved so fast and
allowed lies and secrets and unspoken
words to play a role in their story. The
heart cried louder than before, for the
hurt was to much to bear, a love once
bound for greatness has died. The promise
of everlasting love was gone, tears came
from their heart before their eyes could
show the sadness of knowing that this was
the ending to their love story.

# THE LETTER

I remember when I was all he wanted
but you have him now, he is now taken
by your charms, all my efforts to show
him my love has been refused, you have
his mind and above all you have his heart
knowing all this, I am still very much
in love with him. He has always been
my one and only, I feel helpless knowing
you hold all the cards, so I am asking
you... "Do you love him? Are you enjoying
him because you can?" Please do not break
his heart, if you don't love him, return
him back to me, leave him gracefully if
you cared for him. He is a good man and I
love him more than you ever will, this
man is my heart and my love, I will pick
up the pieces, until he feels the love we once
shared.

# CAN'T SAY

If I can't say goodbye to our love
would anyone know? If I don't
give up on my feelings for you
would my love know I questioned
his feelings? Would he know I feel
lost thinking of you when he holds
me close?" "Would he understand?
I am so torn knowing I can't live
without you both. I know I am the
selfish one, because I can't say goodbye
to you, my darling you are part of me
you came when I discovered who I am, I
don't want to set you free, you were
my first, crazy as it all was I simply
can't say goodbye.

# STRENGTH OF A WOMAN

A woman's strength should never be
questioned, she has the ability to love
and feel like no other, she feels and give
comfort when it's needed, knowing this
was her gift from the beginning of life.
She was crowned a queen from birth, as
she walked through the world, she
understands her role, so she stand tall
and takes her place by embracing her
destiny. As challenges comes, she forgets
how special she really is, and questions
herself, for the power given at times can
be very overwhelming which is what a
great ruler does, however her compassion
confirms why she is a Queen. The softness
of her heart is comforting and her strength
shows us a new world, so we look to her for
guidance, which she gives willingly
without question for she knows without
her presence we would all be lost.

# MY KING

My king revealed himself to me, and
commanded me to know his love, I
wondered why he asked this of me. He
was so strong and ever so gentle, his
presence was something I have never
seen or felt before, but I felt connected
to him all the same. My only wish was
to know why he allowed me in, his
warmth was so comforting and beautiful.
I wanted to drown myself in him, never
have I felt so loved, I wanted to shout how
wonderful he was. He took over my
thoughts my feelings and who I thought
I was. I know that his presence was his
gift to me, and that my heart has
always been his... I will cherish this
moment forever for my father crowned
me his princess today.

# STORY TELLER

His stories caught my attention
they were all of his life lessons.
Looking into his eyes I knew them
to be true, as he spoke his eyes revealed
the love for his family and so much
more. I felt so privileged to be in his
company as I took it all in. Listening
to him I wanted to believe that some
day I could share my stories with others.
In this brief moment I received a
message from the heart ... Always listen
carefully to life's lessons for they are
given to us everyday, if only we choose
to listen. So please listen to the next
story teller, their stories could be a life
changing moment if you allow your
heart to be opened.

# THE OUTSIDER

I watched daily as he turned himself
 inside out to be what the world wanted
him to be, he was waiting for comfort to
 come but it never came. He question his
existence and his choices, thinking
something was wrong with him, and he
continued walking on egg shells, waiting
 for the world to swallow him, judge him,
 hurt him, and indeed all his fears came true.
 The world he wanted to please was greater
than his heart. He felt like as outsider
 around this world. This world he wanted
to be a part of showed no love or
understanding and marveled knowing
 he was lost. I reached my hand out to
my dear friend and told him, hold on, I
 believe in you this is your life, embrace
it, forget about fears and acceptance
 simply breath one day at a time and
 live your life.

# ROSE'S HAPPINESS

The battle was won, finally her inner
fears was free, Rose felt her blinders
disappearing and fell into a great
laughter followed by the deepest cry.
Rose felt her rebirth and embraced it, she
could now see the woman she has always
been and the mother she always wanted
to be. Rose life was now beautiful and she
shined as bright as the stars did at
midnight, another blissfulness moment
was given as she opened the door, beautiful
Rose was given flowers by her new love.
The fragrances reminded her of her rebirth
and she smiled, she now understood how
love felt when given with great meaning.
True love had finally found my sweet Rose
and I happily cheered her on.

# FREE ME

I have given you my all, I can't
remember who I am, or when we began.
I just simply know that I love you
more than I love myself. I feel so lost
without you, and I feel lost in my own
skin. "Please free me!" Loving you
makes me question everything I was
before we met, I know you love toying
with my heart, when you do this, its
hurts more than you will ever know, I
know you don't love me, but can't I
walk away, so again I am pleading
with you... "Please release the hold you
have on me?" "Please free me!"

# FOOLISH

It is said that as time passes, memories will fade for time is a healer when comfort is allowed in, or so we would like to believe. If this is true and time is a healer, what happens to the heart? Does it give in to the power of time? Does the heart forget the many promises made, or words spoken such as... "I will you love forever, my heart is yours always." Is the heart able to forget the hurt? It appears that the heart is stronger than the power of time, or is the heart just simply to foolish to allow time in. Which one do you believe is stronger?

# EVERLASTING

As I opened the door to this house I
wondered why it pulled at me so much.
This house by vision was not inviting
but there was a calling that could not
be ignored, I felt I have entered this house
several times before and asked...What
was happening? My steps led me to
rooms that was familiar to me, the
memories all came rushing back and they
took me over, it all felt like yesterday.
"What was happening?" I asked again.
 "My love you are home he answered... The
journey is over, you have found your way
back to me." I smiled and ran into his arms
through our kisses I whispered "I am happy
you waited"

# TIMING

I recalled your spoken words of regret
and they reached my soul, hurtful as
those words were I respected your
choice and walked away. "Can you
understand why your declaration of
love confuses me? You had my heart
and I may always love you, but the
hurt you freely bestowed on me, reached
my soul, you are not worthy of my heart.
I am moved knowing you love me, however
time did not offer her friendship in our
story, please respect my choice as I did yours.

# THE EMBRACE

He cried and I wanted to comfort him.
"What could have caused this hurt
my love feels?" He reached out his
hands and gently pulled me into his
arms, I remembered him holding me
so tight, then he shared the story of
his always. "His always had found
her way back to him. He told me his
tears was for the hurt that he knew I
would feel. He hoped for her to return
so many times, but never thought it
was possible, she always had ownership
of his heart he said as he held my hand.
He pulled me in again into his arms and
asked for my forgiveness which I gave
with all my heart.

## THE FOOL

Tell me of your love was her plea
say the words I want to believe, tell
me of our love and how beautiful we
were together. Tell me again how much
you missed sharing our love, when we are
apart. I am willing to play the fool. I
can remember the tender moments we
shared, and how it felt when you
whispered my name as you kissed me
over and over again, please say the sweet
words, I want so much to believe in them
now. but you never answer my plea, you
asked if I love you and my reply was
always... "Yes, I love you" but beloved
why couldn't you give me your love?

# THE JOURNEY

When we are young we feel empowered.
Our feelings and thoughts are beyond
anyone's comprehension and we feel
special. The thought of anyone feeling
this way is questioned, because we feel
gifted, but this moment has been embraced
by many before, this feeling can't be
described, however the wise ones knows
that this moment can only be captured
once, so we are allow to marvel in it's
beauty for a short time, this moment, the
feeling that can't be described is the
beginning of another journey, and youth
is the compass that guides us.

# PRIDE

I would like you to meet a dear friend
she has the ability to draw many to
her, she believes she has all the answers
through secretly she knows she is lost.
Watching her closely, I saw a smile
escaped her lips at the enjoyment of
leading others to know her world, she
makes no apologies for her treachery.
She believes that she is special, but her
sadness can be felt through the many
mask she wears, for she knows she is lost
without the presence of someone in her
world, you see my friend wants to keep
herself safe, in doing so she believes she's
untouchable. So allow me to introduce
you to my friend Pride. Her presence is
just as strong as anger and lust.

## PAIN

You don't love me, and you refuse
to, you have torn me apart... I can
see the pleasure in your eyes when I
am hurting. "Why must you only
appear when I am hurting?" I am
good, my heart is so opened... When
happiness is felt, you are not near
to share these moments with me, but
how you love when I am confused
and looking for anything to fulfill
the loneliness I feel. "Why do
you only appear when I am lost?"

# ESCAPE

She was always called upon when
a soothing voice was needed, when
understanding was given with no
question, she always gave comfort
she was your safe haven, she was
your escape. Feeling her lips on
yours was what you needed, with
her you could feel passion. It felt
wonderful getting lost in her arms
being so close you wish never to be
apart. She gave her everything
and you welcomed it all, you have
tried to replace her with others but
she has always been there... "She
is not an obsession, but you know
her name."

# THE POWER OF YOU

There are three simple little words
when said can change lives. These
words when said with great meaning
may cause tears to appear. These
words when said do not show your
weakness, they only show your
strength and your heart, do not
question yourself when you utter
these words, this is your moment
for you are changing, and your
heart is now opened. What are these
three simply words? It's simply
saying: "I am sorry"

# KNOWING

Give it your all, make it your passion.
Know it, embrace it no matter what.
Live it, dream it, make it a part of
you. Let it consume you, breath it,
taste it, smell it, let it drive you.
Make it your only thought, for it's
all a part of who you are, this is your
purpose, this is why you are here, it's
the only thing you understand with
great clarity, this feeling is yours, it's
your gift to share with the world.

# BETRAYAL

Anger had a hold on her now, the world she once looked to has turned dark without a warning. She would not think of love, for love made her weak and feel emotions she was not willing to share or give, so she gave in to darkness. She wanted only to lose herself in moments that she knew she could understand. Sadly these moments brought her no comfort, but she was willing to get lost all the same, in her mind love has never been a friend and she wouldn't give in anymore, so she decided to keep love at a distance and welcomed anger as her companion.

"This is the sad tale of betrayal."

# THE WINDOWS OF A HOUSE

It is said that when one door closes
another opens, but I am a true believer
that windows shows the heart of a house.
To really feel a house you have to open
all the windows and let the house show
its true beauty, every window has a
story, if you open one window the love of
family is felt, the next window reminds
you of regrets and moments lost come to life
but another window let's the sun in and
a new day is felt. If you continue another
window shows growth and understanding.
Finally when the last window is opened the
essence of the house comes alive for the love
felt in this house is timeless.

# GROWTH

From youth the message given was be
kind to others, as we embark on this
journey to life, we do as we are told, we
give love, kindness and understanding
and life moves on, time changes, we
discover who we are. Innocence is lost
and growth shows its various colors.
We discover love, passion, likes and
dislikes, hearts are broken for many
did not get the message given.  Though
regrets will always surface, we are wise
and we want to try again, we thank
the messengers of life lessons for their
knowledge, because without regrets
life would lose its meaning.

# DISAPPOINTMENT

I have been pushed, and misunderstood
my screams has been loud, and still
they were not heard. I wanted to give
you my all. I have said all the right
words but they were not welcomed, I wish
you knew of my pain. Why can't you
see me? This is a bittersweet feeling, the
love I feel for you is a love I can't escape.
My wish is not to be a part of you, and
let you go, hoping maybe I could breath
again on my own. I feel hopeless searching
for a happiness that is hurtful, sadness
is the only friendship I want now, it's my
only comfort.

# DARKNESS TAKES OVER

Welcome to darkness little one, how
lost you must feel now, I know you
can feel the walls closing in on you
now, darkness wants to dance with
you tonight, I want to feel your warmth
for it feels so cold inside, I am your
everything now, do that sweet rag doll
dance they all do for me before the end
comes. I want to see the confusion and
acceptances in your eyes, knowing you
feel lost means everything to me, I have
you now little one, you are all mine.
Welcome to my world, welcome home.

# THE VICTIM

The world opened it's arms to her and
yet she was not willing to feel it's
comfort, kindness was given and it was
used, lessons learned from the past was
shared and again it was used because
it could be. The gift of friendship was
given out of kindness and it was used
because it could be. I call the takers of
all these treasures a victim, for this
was her name, she loved playing the
role, this was all she really knew, this
was her only way to feel special.

# WHAT WOULD YOU DO FOR LOVE

What would you do when every time
you knock on a door, it's closes over
and over again. "Would you welcome
any reply, good or bad?" Could the
heart break you feel be placed into words?
This love is a love that can't be forgotten
for it's a everlasting love, it's a part of
you, it's who you are. This love can bring
you to your knees, for without this love, you
know you are empty. "What would you do
for love?" would you sell your soul to have
this love again?

"What would you do for love?"

# FALLEN ANGEL

I looked into her eyes and saw an
emptiness that made me feel hollow
when she spoke my heart cried. This
angel was lost. She was so taken in
by the world, her voice was lost and
the dreams that turned little girls into
women was gone. This sad angel never
had dreams, she always felt alone, for
no one told her she was beautiful or
special. She was a fallen soul, and
I felt her sadness, but I truly believe
someday she will know how special
she really is, this is my wish for this
angel.

## MISSING YOU ALWAYS

When hands are held it's a feeling
of comfort, it's a moment that says
I am here and I care, my hands was
held by a very special woman. This
woman was beautiful and kind.
knowing I held her hand brings tears
to my soul, how I wish I could hold
her hand for just one second, if I had
this one wish I would hold on tight.
This amazing woman saw something
in me that I am just starting to
understand, the words she said and
the love she gave still moves me. My
hope is to be as strong and amazing
as she saw I could be. I miss you.


For my beloved Lavender

# HAPPY ENDING

The unthinkable has happened, the
unexpected has happened, this is a
happy moment, and it's not a dream.
The heart and mind are finally in
agreement, words are happy that they
were spoken... Beauty was thrilled
that she could play her part, Time
allowed herself to be kind; Touch
played her role wonderfully as she
always does, allowing this beautiful
moment to happen. They all kept
pain, envy, and betrayal at a distance.
This moment was everything for they
knew uniting would give a happy
ending to a great love story. Don't
take this moment lightly for happy
endings to a great story only happens
when true love is felt.